baby-sitters
little sister

#2

Karen's
Roller
Skates

**Other books by
Ann M. Martin**

P. S. Longer Letter Later
(written with Paula Danziger)
Leo the Magnificat
Rachel Parker, Kindergarten Show-off
Eleven Kids, One Summer
Ma and Pa Dracula
Yours Turly, Shirley
Ten Kids, No Pets
With You and Without You
Me and Katie (the Pest)
Stage Fright
Inside Out
Bummer Summer

For older readers:

Missing Since Monday
Just a Summer Romance
Slam Book

THE BABY-SITTERS CLUB series
THE BABY-SITTERS CLUB mysteries
THE KIDS IN MS. COLMAN'S CLASS series
BABY-SITTERS LITTLE SISTER series
(see inside book covers for a complete listing)

#2

Karen's
Roller
Skates

ANN M. MARTIN

Illustrations by Susan Tang

A
LITTLE
APPLE
PAPERBACK

SCHOLASTIC INC.

New York Toronto London Auckland Sydney
Mexico City New Delhi Hong Kong Buenos Aires

This book is in
loving memory of my grandmother
Adele Read Martin
August 2, 1894 – April 18, 1988

ISBN 0-439-35196-0

12 11 10 9 8 7 6 5 4 3 2 1   1 2 3 4 5 6/0

Printed in the U.S.A.   40

First Scholastic printing, revised edition, October 2001

Daredevil

"Look out! Look out! Coming through!" I shouted.

I was on my new roller skates. I was skating fast.

My little brother Andrew and my friend Nancy Dawes were on the sidewalk. They were not on roller skates. It was easier for them to jump out of my way than for me to stop.

I am Karen Brewer. I am almost seven. I am a world champion skater. Well, maybe not a *world* champion skater. Well, maybe not a champion at all. But I am good. Very good.

I got my skates a few weeks ago. I just knew I would like skating. Here are the things I can do:

1. Skate forward
2. Skate forward fast
3. Skate backward (not so fast)
4. Turn around
5. Stop without falling down
6. Try any trick I see

Actually I am not really allowed to do number six. I can do *some* tricks I see, but my parents don't like me to try *every* one. Daddy says, "You are a daredevil, Karen. Be careful when you're skating. We don't want any broken bones."

Maybe I am a daredevil. I like to try tricks. I like to try jumping and spinning. I like to leap over things. I like to fly over humps in the sidewalk.

This is what I wear when I skate: shorts with a stripe up each leg; red-and-white-striped socks; a red-and-white jersey; a red headband; wrist guards; knee pads; and of course, my skates.

My skates are so, so cool. They are red. They are the lace-up kind. The wheels are yellow. (Nancy says they won't be yellow for long.)

I love my skates.

"Coming through!" I yelled again.

Nancy and Andrew jumped away. We have had a couple of small accidents. Maybe that's why Daddy calls me a daredevil. Maybe that's why he warns me to be careful.

I try to remember to be careful, but sometimes I forget. It is fun to go fast. It is fun to jump. When I go fast, I feel like I'm flying. When I do a trick, I feel breathless and happy.

"Karen! Andrew! Time to come in!" That was our mother.

"Nancy! Time for you to come in, too."

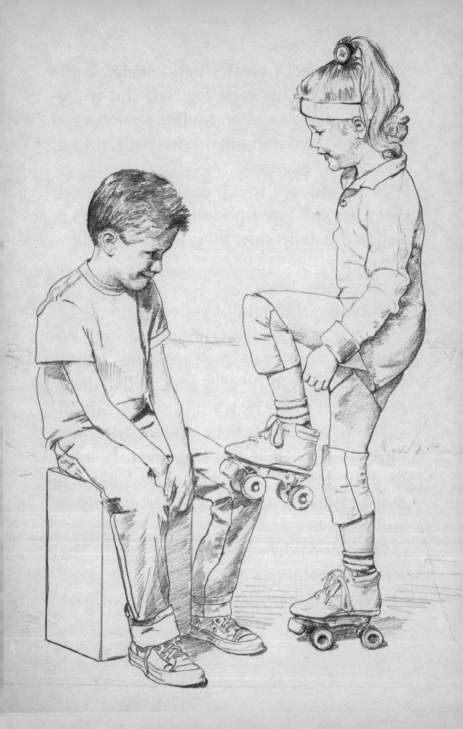

That was Mrs. Dawes. Nancy lives next door to Mommy's house.

It was a Thursday afternoon. Mrs. Dawes wanted Nancy to come in because it was time for dinner. Mommy wanted Andrew and me to come in because it was time to go to Daddy's.

My mommy and daddy are divorced. Andrew and I live at our daddy's every other weekend and for two weeks in the summer. The rest of the time we live at our mommy's. Usually we go to Daddy's on Friday afternoon. But that weekend we were going a day early. Mommy and Seth were taking a vacation. (Seth is our stepfather.) They would be away for three days. They were going to the state of Maine.

" 'Bye, Nancy," I said. "See you in school tomorrow."

" 'Bye, Karen. 'Bye, Andrew," Nancy replied.

I skated up my driveway as fast as I could go. Andrew ran behind me. We were sorry we weren't going to the state of Maine. But going to Daddy's was almost as good. I would bring my skates with me.

I was looking forward to a weekend of roller-skating.

There was a new trick I wanted to try.

Saturday Morning

Stretch, stretch, stretch.

Yawn.

Sometimes it is hard to wake up. But not on a Saturday morning. On a Saturday morning you can roll around in bed. You can scrunch up the pillow. You can kiss your stuffed animals. But you do not have to get up unless you want to.

I lay in my bed. I was sooooo happy it was Saturday. I kicked the covers back. Then I looked around for Moosie, my stuffed cat, and Tickly, my blanket. I found them on the floor.

"Sorry, Moosie. Sorry, Tickly," I said. I picked them up and hugged them.

I don't get to see Moosie very often. See, I have two of almost everything, one for Daddy's house, one for Mommy's house. That way, when Andrew and I go to Daddy's, we hardly have to bring anything with us. Since Moosie stays at Daddy's, I only see him every other weekend. Andrew

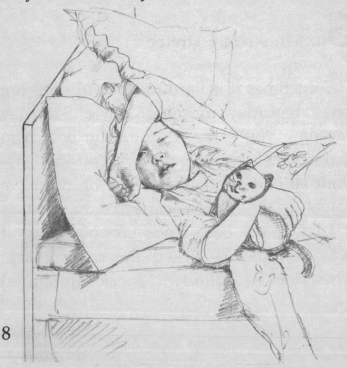

and I have clothes and toys and books at Daddy's, too. We have other clothes and toys and books at Mommy's. (Actually, for a long time, I had only one Tickly. But I forgot Tickly so many times going back and forth between Mommy's and Daddy's, that finally I just ripped him in half. Now I have half of Tickly at the big house and half of Tickly at the little house.)

The big house is Daddy's. It really is a big house. And lots of people live in it. There's Daddy and my stepmother, Elizabeth. There are Elizabeth's four kids. Sam and Charlie are very old. They are in high school. Kristy is younger. She's thirteen. She baby-sits. I just love Kristy. I'm glad she's my big sister. David Michael is almost my age. He's seven. As soon as I have my birthday, I'll catch up to him.

Guess who else lives in the big house? Shannon and Boo-Boo. Shannon is David Michael's puppy. Well, she's really everybody's puppy, but *mostly* she's David Michael's. Boo-Boo is Daddy's old fat cat. I don't like him much. He does not do a thing except eat, sleep, meow, and claw the furniture.

Do you want to hear something spooky? Next door to the big house lives a witch. Really! Cross my heart. Most people think she is just an old woman named Mrs. Porter. But I know she is a witch. Her witch name is Morbidda Destiny. She has a weird cat named Midnight. She grows magic herbs in a garden in her backyard. And several times I have seen her with a broom.

My big-house best friend is Hannie Papadakis. She lives across the street and one house down. Hannie and Nancy Dawes and I are in the same class in school. (Since we go to private school and David Michael goes to public school, I only see him every other weekend. He can be a pain, so I don't mind this too much.)

The little house is Mommy's. It really is a little house, and the only people who live there are Mommy and Seth and Andrew and me. Plus, Seth has a dog named Midgie and a cat named Rocky.

Nancy Dawes is my little-house best friend.

I like all the people at both houses, and *most* of the animals. So does Andrew. But sometimes we wish that our parents were not divorced and that we lived in just one house.

"Then I could see you every day," I said to Moosie.

At last I got up. I put my skating outfit on. I ran downstairs to eat breakfast. It was a beautiful day. I wanted to try my new roller-skating trick.

Oops!

As soon as breakfast was over, I put on my skates. I do not have two pairs of skates. I do not have two skating outfits. So I have to remember to bring my skates and skating clothes with me when I go to Mommy's or to Daddy's.

It is a pain in the neck.

I am not allowed to wear my roller skates indoors. That is a rule at the big house. It is also a rule at the little house.

I carried my skates outdoors and sat down

on the steps in front of the house. I put one foot in one skate.

"Karen!" called Elizabeth.

"Yes?" I answered. "I'm out front."

Elizabeth came to the door. She was holding Shannon's leash. "Honey, would you take Shannon for a walk, please?"

I did not know what to do. I was getting ready to go skating. But I wanted to walk Shannon, too. Then I got an idea.

"Sure!" I replied.

Elizabeth handed me the leash. I took off my skate and came back inside.

"Thanks, Karen," said Elizabeth.

"You're welcome. . . . Hey, Andrew!" I called.

Andrew came running.

"Want to help me walk Shannon?" I asked him. "I've got a great idea. I know how we can walk Shannon, *and* I can roller-skate, *and* you can ride your trike."

"How?" asked Andrew.

"Like this." I fastened Shannon's leash

to her collar. Then I gave the leash to my brother. "You can ride your trike and let Shannon run beside you," I told him. "I'll skate ahead of you so Shannon doesn't get tangled up with me. Okay?"

"Okay," said Andrew.

We got Andrew's big-house trike out of the garage. He sat on it and I gave him Shannon's leash.

Then I sat on the sidewalk and put my skates on. I remembered that I had left my wrist guards in the house. Oh, well, I thought. I don't really need them.

"Ready, set, go!" I cried.

I charged down the sidewalk. Andrew was behind me. He traveled more slowly. Shannon ran next to him. Andrew was careful that Shannon stayed away from the wheels of his trike.

ZOOM! I whizzed along until I could coast. I saw a hump in the sidewalk ahead of me. Goody! I sailed over it. Maybe someday I will be a skier and go flying through the air off ski jumps.

14

When I reached the driveway of the house next door, I skidded to a halt. Andrew stopped behind me.

"Woof!" said Shannon.

Andrew and I turned around. I skated back to our driveway. Suddenly I remembered the trick I wanted to try.

"Hey, Andrew!" I said. "Want to see a really cool trick?"

"Sure!" replied Andrew. He loves tricks. Magic tricks, skating tricks, diving tricks, any kind of tricks. Even April Fools' Day tricks.

"Okay," I said. "I'll be right back."

I skated into our garage. On a shelf I found two empty coffee cans. Perfect. I skated back to the sidewalk and set the cans down next to each other.

"I," I announced to Andrew, "am going to leap over these cans. I saw a woman on TV do it. She leaped over *six*. But I will try just two."

"Oh, Karen," said Andrew. "Do you think you should?" He had stopped his

16

trike and was sitting still. He looked very worried.

I felt sort of nervous myself. But I just had to try the trick. I backed away from the cans. Then I skated forward as fast as I could. When I got near the cans, I jumped up, soared over them, and landed on my feet. I could hardly believe it.

"I did it!" I shouted.

"Hurray!" yelled Andrew.

I turned around to grin at him. That was when I lost my balance. My feet shot out from under me. I put my hands out as I fell. I landed on them hard.

"Ow, ow, ow!" I cried. "Andrew, I'm hurt!"

Broken Wrist

My bottom hurt where I'd sat down on it. But my right wrist hurt more. I looked at it.

I screamed.

My wrist was bent back at a funny angle. I couldn't wiggle my fingers. When I tried to move my wrist, it hurt so much I gasped.

"Andrew, my wrist is broken!" I cried.

Andrew jumped off his trike. He and Shannon ran to me. When he saw my wrist, he began to cry. "Oh, Karen!" he said.

"Get Daddy," I whispered to him.

Andrew left Shannon with me to keep me company. Then he ran into the house. I had never seen him run so fast.

I sat on the sidewalk and tried not to look at my wrist. I could not help crying, though. Shannon put her paws on my shoulder and licked my tears away.

"Thank you, Shannon," I said in a wavery voice.

"Karen!" Daddy called. He and Kristy came running out of the house. Daddy

19

reached me first. He took one look at my wrist. Then he gathered me into his arms very gently.

"Does this hurt? Does this hurt?" he asked as he picked me up.

"Just don't shake me around, okay?" I replied.

Daddy walked carefully back into the house. Kristy held onto my left hand, the one that wasn't hurt.

"I should have worn my wrist guards," I said. I sniffled loudly.

"Don't worry about that now," said Daddy.

Elizabeth met us at the front door. She held it open and Daddy carried me inside. He laid me on the couch in the living room.

"It's broken," I said. "My wrist is broken."

Elizabeth looked pale. "Yes, you're right, honey. I'll go call Doctor Dellenkamp."

While Elizabeth called the doctor, Daddy and Kristy and Andrew sat with me on the couch. Kristy was still holding my hand.

She made me smile by singing a song about a baby bumblebee.

Soon Elizabeth came back.

"Karen, honey," she said, "Doctor Dellenkamp wants you to go to the hospital. She'll meet us in the emergency room. Kristy, you stay here with Andrew and David Michael. Sam and Charlie are out."

"No," said Kristy firmly. "I'm going to the hospital with Karen."

Kristy and her mother looked at each other for a long time.

At last Elizabeth said, "Okay. You go. I'll stay here."

"Thanks, Mom," said Kristy. She gave Elizabeth a kiss.

I like Elizabeth, but I was glad Kristy was coming to the hospital with us. She is the best, best big sister ever.

Daddy carried me out to Elizabeth's station wagon. "We'll take this car," he said. "You can lie down in the back."

"And I'll sit with you," Kristy added.

Elizabeth covered me with a blanket. "I'll see you soon, sweetie," she said. "I know everything will be all right. And don't try to be brave. Scream and yell and give Doctor Dellenkamp a hard time if you feel like it."

I managed to giggle. "Okay," I said. Sometimes Elizabeth is funny.

Daddy pulled out of the driveway. He pulled out so fast that the tires squealed. Then he raced through Stoneybrook to the hospital.

"There's the emergency entrance!" Kristy called.

Daddy zoomed in. I began to feel scared. My wrist hurt. And I'd never been in a hospital before.

Emergency!

Daddy parked the station wagon. He parked it near the wide double doors that were under the EMERGENCY sign. Then he carried me through the doors and down a hallway. Kristy walked with us.

"Did I ever tell you about the time I broke my ankle?" she asked.

I nodded. I was beginning to cry again. I did not like the way the hospital smelled. It smelled like medicine. Yucky, bad medicine.

Before Kristy could tell the story again,

we came to a desk. A lady was sitting behind it. "Oh, my goodness," she said when she saw my wrist.

"Is Doctor Dellenkamp here yet?" asked Daddy. "I'm Watson Brewer and this is my daughter Karen. Doctor Dellenkamp said she would meet us at the hospital."

"Here I am!"

I heard Dr. Dellenkamp's voice in the hall behind us. Usually I do not like to hear her voice. This is because her voice is usually saying, "Okay, Karen, time for a shot." But just then I was glad to hear it. Dr. Dellenkamp was going to make my wrist better.

That's what I thought. But the first thing she said was, "Karen, I won't be setting your wrist. We'll have to wait for the bone doctor. Fixing bones is his specialty. That's what he does best. He should be here soon. While we're waiting for him, you can go to the X-ray room. We need some pictures of your wrist bones. And Mr. Brewer, I need you to fill out some forms."

A nurse rolled a wheelchair over to us. "Here is your chariot," she said to me. "And I am your chariot driver. I will take you to X ray."

"All by myself?" I said. I wasn't sure what X ray was, and I didn't want to go there. "Do I *have* to go?" I asked.

"Yes," Dr. Dellenkamp told me. "Kristy can go with you. How would that be?"

Kristy looked at me. "Okay?" she said. "Your daddy has to fill out forms. Besides, I want to watch. I love hospital stuff."

I thought Kristy was crazy. But if she would come with me, I would go to X ray. "Okay," I said.

Daddy put me in the wheelchair.

"Off we go," said the nurse. "When we're finished, I'll bring you back to your dad."

The nurse pushed me down a hallway. I had never sat in a wheelchair. Everyone in the hall looked at me. I began to feel sort of important. The nurse pushed me into a little room with a lot of machines in it. A man wearing a white jacket and white pants was in the room. He looked like a doctor — and not like a doctor. There was no stethoscope around his neck.

"Hi, there," he said. "I am Tom. I am the X-ray technician. I am going to take pictures of the inside of your wrist — of your wrist bones."

"Yuck," I said.

Tom rested my arm on a table. He covered me with a bib that felt very heavy.

"What's this for?" I asked.

"It's to protect you from the X rays. We only want them near your wrist. Don't worry. I know what I'm doing."

Then he moved one of those machines right up to my wrist. *Click* went the machine.

"The biggest camera in the world," said Kristy, who was standing in the doorway, watching.

I giggled.

Tom started moving my arm around and taking more pictures. *Click, click, click.* Sometimes it hurt to move my arm, so Tom tried

26

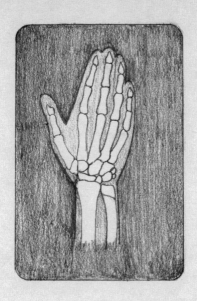

to be very careful. And I tried not to cry.
Tom was nice.

"All finished," Tom said soon. He took
off the bib.

"Now what?" I asked.

"Your chariot will take you back to your
father," said the nurse.

"Good-bye, Karen!" called Tom. "Feel
better."

"Good-bye," I replied. "Thank you."

It was time to wait for the bone doctor.

The Bone Doctor

The nurse pushed me back to Daddy.

"Tom took pictures of my bones," I told him. "Are you finished with those papers?"

"All finished," said Daddy.

Dr. Dellenkamp showed us into a little room nearby. Well, it *felt* like a room, but it wasn't really one. The walls were just curtains. There was a long row of those rooms. You could pull the curtains open — or close them up.

Dr. Dellenkamp closed ours. She and Daddy helped me out of the wheelchair.

They sat me on a table that looked like a high bed. Then Dr. Dellenkamp said, "The bone doctor will be here soon. His name is Doctor Humphrey. He's looking at your X rays now, Karen. I'm going to go look at them, too."

Dr. Dellenkamp pushed through the curtains and left.

As soon as she was gone I said, "I'm bored."

Daddy and Kristy laughed.

Kristy told me three elephant jokes. Daddy began to sing a silly song about marching ants. But then the curtain opened. A man with a mustache came into the room.

"Are you the bone doctor?" I asked him.

"Yes," he replied. He smiled. "I am Doctor Humphrey. You must be Karen Brewer."

Daddy introduced himself and Kristy. Then Dr. Humphrey explained what he was going to do. I didn't like the sound of it. The very first thing was a shot.

"OW!" I screeched.

"All over," said Dr. Humphrey. "Now

your wrist won't hurt for awhile."

He and Daddy helped me to lie down. I began to feel very relaxed and a little sleepy. Dr. Humphrey picked up my arm. It was the one with the broken wrist, but it didn't hurt a bit.

A tall pole was standing by the bed. There were some metal tubes hanging from it. The doctor put my fingers in them. When he let go, my fingers dropped down a little, but they stayed in the tubes. The tubes held them tight! They were like a magic trick that Andrew used to have. If you stuck your pointer fingers into the ends of this straw tube and then pulled them apart — they got stuck. But if you pushed them together, the tube loosened and you could get your fingers out again.

"Hey, cool!" cried Kristy. She was watching my arm as it hung from the metal tubes. "I just saw all your bones go back where they belong. Your wrist doesn't look broken anymore."

"That's right," said Dr. Humphrey. "Now it's time to put the cast on."

Dr. Humphrey wrapped cotton around and around my hand, my wrist, and right up over my elbow. Then he wrapped my arm with wet white bandages. The bandages dried fast. As they dried, they hardened into a cast. Dr. Humphrey took my fingers out of the tubes and gave me my arm back. It weighed a ton. That cast was *heavy*.

"How do you feel, Karen?" asked Daddy.

"Fine," I said. "A little sleepy."

"Good," said Dr. Humphrey. "Now Tom just has to take a few more pictures of your wrist. We need to make sure the bones are in the right places. After that, you can go home."

So I visited Tom one more time. The nurse pushed me around in my chariot again. When Tom was done taking the pictures, Dr. Dellenkamp talked to Daddy for a few minutes. Then she handed me a white sling. She rested my cast in the bottom part and put the top part around my neck.

"Now your arm won't feel so heavy," she said.

The nurse wheeled me outside and Daddy drove the car over to us. He and Kristy helped me to lie down in the back.

I was still sleepy. And I was having bad thoughts — like how would I button buttons or feed Shannon and Boo-Boo or Rocky and Midgie with just one hand?

I began to feel very, very sorry for myself.

Tea and TV

Daddy steered the car into our driveway. Home again. He parked the car. Then he came around to the back.

"Do you think you can walk inside?" he asked me.

"No," I said crossly. "I am too tired. And my arm hurts."

Daddy carried me into the house.

"Karen! Karen!" Andrew cried. He and David Michael opened the front door for us. "How is your wrist? Does it hurt? Did you cry? What did the doctor do?"

I showed them my cast. I put on the saddest face I could make.

"Poor Karen," said Elizabeth.

She had met us in the hallway. Sam and Charlie were with her. My big brothers had come home while I was at the hospital.

"Hey, Karen, we fixed you a place in the den," said Sam.

"You can spend the rest of the afternoon there," added Charlie.

"Yeah," said Andrew. "We put pillows there, and a blanket, and your books. We'll take care of you."

"I'll let Shannon stay with you," David Michael offered.

"Okay," I said in a teeny-tiny voice.

Daddy carried me into the den and laid me on the couch. Kristy fluffed my pillows. Elizabeth covered me with the blanket. Andrew handed me my favorite book, *The Witch Next Door*.

"Thank you," I said in my very small voice, "but I can't read this now. I don't feel well."

"How about calling Mommy?" Daddy suggested. "That might make you feel better. We have to tell her about your accident, anyway."

So we called Mommy in the state of Maine. I talked to her for a long time. I told her about the hospital. Then I talked to Seth. When I hung up, I did feel better.

Sam and Charlie and Daddy and Elizabeth had left the room, but everyone else was still there. "What's on TV?" I asked.

David Michael jumped up. "*I'll* check," he said importantly. He found the remote control and switched the channels for me. We found some good cartoons.

"I'm hungry," I said after awhile.

Kristy told Elizabeth, and Elizabeth fixed me a special lunch. She even made tea. For dessert, Charlie gave me a candy bar.

"Wow!" I said. "Thanks."

All afternoon I played on the couch. I didn't feel sleepy anymore, and my wrist didn't hurt — much. I leaned against my pillows. I felt like a princess. I asked for hundreds of things.

But near dinnertime when I said, "Hey, Andrew, get me my coloring book," Andrew replied, "No. I'm busy."

"David Michael, *you* get my coloring book," I ordered.

"Get it yourself," he replied. "You can walk."

"Hmphh," I said. But I did get it myself. Only it wasn't any fun coloring with my left hand.

When dinner was ready, Elizabeth said, "Come sit with us at the table, Karen. It's time to eat."

"Can't I eat on the couch?" I asked.

"Do you need to?"

"No." I was feeling fine.

Everyone must have known I was fine. After dinner, David Michael got to watch *his* favorite program on TV and Charlie didn't even give me another candy bar.

By bedtime I was cross again. "I'm not

sleepy," I complained to Daddy and Elizabeth.

"Well, try going to sleep anyway," they replied.

So I did, even though I could only hold Tickly. Moosie had to rest beside me.

Back to the Hospital

When I woke up the next morning, I didn't feel cross anymore. I didn't feel sleepy and my wrist only hurt a little. Outside, the sun was shining.

"Well," I said to Moosie, "I am not going to waste *this* day lying around on the couch. I am going to play outside. There's nothing wrong with my legs. Maybe I could even go skating later."

I got out of bed. I took off my nightgown. It wasn't easy, with only one hand. Last night, Kristy had helped me to get undressed and put my nightgown on.

"But today," I told Moosie, "I am going to do everything by myself. I don't need any help."

I decided to wear my blue jeans, my moccasins, and my pink shirt with the unicorn on front. It took a long, long time, but I pulled on the jeans and the shirt.

"I did it!" I told Moosie. I felt like I was two years old and just learning to get dressed. Of course, when I was two, I wasn't wearing a cast that weighed a ton. And I could use both hands. Today was different.

I slipped my feet into my moccasins. That was easy. Then I brushed my hair using my left hand. That was *pretty* easy. Then I went downstairs.

"Why, Karen," Elizabeth exclaimed. "Who helped you get dressed? I thought Kristy was still asleep."

"She is," I replied. I sat down at the table. "I did it myself. I can do anything."

Elizabeth raised her eyebrows. She looked at Daddy.

"You can*not* do anything," said David Michael. He and Andrew were sitting at the table with Daddy and Elizabeth.

"I can too." To prove it, I put a piece of bread in the toaster, left-handed. When it popped up, I buttered it, left-handed. The buttering took longer than usual — but I did it.

"See?" I said to David Michael.

David Michael stuck his tongue out at me.

I stuck mine out at him.

"Okay, okay," said Daddy. "Karen, you must be feeling better."

"I'm fine!" I replied. I smiled. If I wanted to go roller-skating, I better look fine.

"I know one thing you can't do," David Michael spoke up. "I bet you can't use the can opener. I bet you can't feed Boo-Boo."

"We'll just see," I said, jumping up.

But David Michael was right. I couldn't use the can opener. I needed two hands for that.

"Well, that's the *only* thing I can't do," I said as I sat down again. "I can dress myself, I can brush my hair, I can eat." I paused. Then I added carefully, "I'm *sure* I can go roller-skating."

"Oh, no you can't!" said Daddy.

"But I didn't break my legs," I pointed out. "Just my wrist."

Daddy shook his head. "No roller-skating. Not for a long time," he said. "If you fell now, you could really hurt your wrist. Besides, your cast is heavy. You might not realize it, but you're off balance. Or you would be if you were on skates."

"Aw, *Daddy*," I said.

"Anyway," he went on, "you have to go back to the hospital this morning. Doctor Humphrey wants to check your cast. Tom might even take another X ray."

"Back to the *hospital?*" I cried. "I don't want to go!"

Waiting

I had to go anyway. Back to the hospital. What a pain.

And Daddy wanted to go very soon. "We don't have an appointment," he said. "We're just supposed to go to the emergency room this morning and wait until Doctor Humphrey can see you. If we go early, maybe we won't have to wait too long."

We left so early that Kristy was *still* asleep. Darn it. I wanted her to come with us. She thinks up good games when you have to do a lot of waiting.

"Can I come?" asked Andrew.

"Well," said Daddy, "I guess so. It's not going to be much fun, though. We'll just be sitting and waiting."

"I want to see the hospital," Andrew said. "Hospitals are instristing."

"Interesting," I corrected him.

"Can I go?" Andrew asked again.

"Sure," replied Daddy.

So Andrew came with us. Daddy drove to the hospital. This time he didn't have to park in the emergency lot, and I could walk into the hospital by myself.

"How come we're going to the emergency room?" I asked Daddy. "I'm not an emergency now."

"Because Doctor Humphrey doesn't have an office like Doctor Dellenkamp does. He just fixes bones, and he does it here in the hospital."

I nodded. Andrew and I sat down in hard plastic chairs in the waiting room. Daddy told the nurse we were there.

"WAHHH!"

Andrew and I turned around fast. Who was crying?

We saw a woman carrying a little girl through the doors under the EMERGENCY sign. The woman was running and the girl was screeching.

"She burned her hand!" the woman told a nurse.

The nurse grabbed a bunch of papers for the woman to sign. Then she took the lady and the little girl into one of those rooms with curtains for walls.

OOOO-EEEE-OOOO. An ambulance came speeding into the emergency parking lot. It pulled right up to the doors of the hospital.

"Andrew! Look!" I cried.

Andrew and I ran to a window. We watched the back of the ambulance open up. Then three men and a woman lifted a stretcher out. They wheeled it inside in a hurry. It flew by us so fast we couldn't even see who was on the stretcher.

"Hey," I said. "Let's play hospital, Andrew. It will be a good waiting game."

"Okay. How do we play?"

"You be the sick person and I'll be the doctor," I told my brother. "You come to my hospital and I'll fix you up."

"What's the matter with me?" asked Andrew.

"Whatever you want."

First Andrew had a broken leg.

"Hmm, I think you need a cast."

Andrew put his leg in my lap and I pretended to make a cast for it.

"Now I have a very very very very sore throat," said Andrew.

I looked down his throat. "You need this medicine," I told him. "It tastes yucky, but you have to take it seventeen times a day. Then your throat will get better."

"Thank you," said Andrew. "Now . . . now I have a big cut on my hand. It's bleeding."

"Ew," I replied. "Okay. First we put this goop on it. Then this Band-Aid. Then — "

"Karen Brewer?" said a nurse.

"She's right here," Daddy answered. He and Andrew and I stood up. Daddy held my unbroken hand.

Boo, I thought. Doctor-time again.

10

The Bone Doctor Again

The nurse showed Daddy and Andrew and me into one of the curtain rooms. I could hear the little girl with the burned hand crying. She was not far away.

"Okay," said the nurse. "Sit right up here on the table." She boosted me up.

"Do I have to get another shot?" I asked her nervously.

The nurse smiled. "Nope. Not this time. Now just wait a few minutes and Doctor Humphrey will be in."

Daddy and Andrew sat in chairs by the table. Andrew looked all around. "This is like a real doctor's office," he said. "I see bandages and those funny scissors and medicine for cuts."

"That medicine is called Merthiolate," I said importantly. I knew that from the time the school nurse had come to our classroom to tell us about first aid.

"Very good! Maybe you'll grow up to be a doctor, Karen Brewer." Dr. Humphrey was pushing aside the curtain. He and Daddy said good-morning to each other. Then Dr. Humphrey looked at my cast. He turned it over and around. "Does this hurt?" he kept asking.

"No . . . no . . . no . . . YES! OW!" Darn that old doctor for hurting me.

"Sorry," he said. "Karen, tell me how you broke your wrist."

"Okay," I replied. "I was roller-skating on our sidewalk. I set up four coffee cans and I jumped over all of them. I landed perfectly." I paused. I knew that wasn't what had really happened, but I was too embarrassed to say that I fell when I was just trying to turn around. After all, I was supposed to be a good skater. I didn't want people to think I couldn't even turn around without falling. I decided to add something else to my story. "It was my best trick ever. I even twirled around in the air," I said.

"Karen — " Andrew began.

"But," I went on, "just after I landed I saw this big caterpillar on the sidewalk."

"Caterpillar?" repeated Daddy. He frowned.

"I didn't want to squish it," I said, "so I tried to leap around it. But I lost my balance. My feet went out from under me, and I put my hands out like this — " (I showed Dr. Humphrey with my good hand) " — and I landed on them. And *crunch*, my right wrist broke."

"There weren't four cans," Andrew said, but no one heard him.

"Hmm," said Dr. Humphrey. "Best way I can think of to break a wrist. Well, it's time for Tom to take some more pictures. We need to see if your bones are doing what they're supposed to be doing."

"More X rays," I said. I sighed.

This time, Andrew came with me to visit Tom. Daddy stayed behind to talk to Dr. Humphrey. When I was done, a nurse took Andrew and me back to Daddy. She handed my X rays to the doctor.

Dr. Humphrey clipped them to a lighted board. He looked at them for a long time. So did I. Funny black-and-white pictures. I could see my arm bones and all my finger bones. (There were lots of them.)

"Well," said Dr. Humphrey. "Hmm. Here's what I think is going to happen. For a couple of weeks, you'll come to the emergency room every Wednesday afternoon. Tom will take X rays. After two weeks, we'll remove this big cast. We'll put a smaller one on. It will be lighter and more comfortable. Then you will only have to have X rays once every two weeks. And eight weeks from now, we'll take your cast off for good." Dr. Humphrey smiled.

But I burst into tears. "Eight weeks!" I cried. "That's a long time."

"Well, yes it is," Daddy said. "It's two months."

I cried even harder. Dr. Humphrey gave me a Kleenex.

"I don't want to wear this for two months. I want to go roller-skating."

"Not until your wrist has healed," the doctor told me.

"Boo," I said. I blew my nose. Then I thought of something. "Will I be able to go to school?" I asked.

"Oh, yes. In a few days, your wrist won't hurt at all. You'll be able to hold a pencil and write, even with the cast on."

Darn. I'd been hoping for a vacation.

Yesterday, I thought, had been a bad day. But today was even worse. No roller-skating for two months — and I had to go to school anyway.

Ricky's Cast

"Good-bye, Karen!" Dr. Humphrey called as Daddy and Andrew and I left.

" 'Bye," I replied glumly.

We walked back to the waiting room.

"Look, Karen. There's a boy with a cast just like yours," said Andrew. "Only his is on his foot."

I was feeling very sorry for myself, so I was staring at the ground. But I glanced up. Then I opened my eyes wide.

"Daddy!" I whispered loudly. I tugged at his shirt, but I didn't point. Pointing is not polite. "I know that boy! That's Ricky. He's in my class."

"Hi, Karen," called Ricky. "Look! I broke my ankle!" he said.

"I broke my wrist," I told him. "How did you break your ankle?"

"I fell down the stairs. How did you break your wrist?"

"Roller-skating."

Daddy and Andrew and I walked over to Ricky Torres and his parents. Daddy started talking to Mr. and Mrs. Torres. Since he was busy, I said to Ricky, "I was doing a roller-skating trick. I jumped over five cans lined up on the sidewalk. I did a double twist in the air. Then I landed. It was perfect." There. That was even better. I didn't want the kids in my class to know what had really happened.

"Karen," said Andrew.

I ignored him. "It was perfect except that I saw this caterpillar and her baby caterpillar and — Hey!"

I was so busy talking that I hadn't noticed

something important. It was Ricky's cast. It was covered with people's names and funny sayings, all written with different pens. Ricky's cast looked like an autograph book. I leaned over to see it better. Someone had written,

2 Ys U R,
2 Ys U B,
I C U R
2 Ys 4 me.

"Cool!" I cried. "What's all this stuff on your cast? Who wrote it?"

"My friends and my mom and dad and brother and sister."

"But — but when did you break your ankle?" I asked. I could not figure out how Ricky had had time to show his cast to so many people.

"I broke it on Friday. Right after school."

Oh. Ricky had been able to show his cast around all day Saturday.

"Is Doctor Humphrey your bone doctor?" I asked.

"Yup. Is he yours?"

"Yup. How long do you have to wear your cast?"

"Six weeks," said Ricky. "How about you?"

"Eight weeks. My broken bone must be worse than yours," I said proudly.

"I guess so." Ricky narrowed his eyes. "Boy, I can't wait for school tomorrow. Everyone will crowd around to see my cast."

"Mine, too!" I cried. "They'll want to see mine, too!"

"But they'll want to see mine more," Ricky told me. "Mine is more interesting. And you know what? By tomorrow morning, I will have Hubert Gregory's signature."

"The baseball player?!" I exclaimed. "He's famous! How are you going to get him to sign your cast?"

"He's my dad's friend," said Ricky. He grinned at me.

I could not grin back.

"Well, we better be going," spoke up Daddy. "Karen, say good-bye to Ricky."

" 'Bye, Ricky."

" 'Bye, Karen."

Boy, I thought. I had plenty to do that afternoon. I had to get people to sign my cast. I had to get *lots* of people to sign it! I couldn't let Ricky go to school with a better cast than mine. But how could I get a signature that was as good as Hubert Gregory's? I didn't know anyone famous.

"Daddy," I said as we were driving home, "I am going to be very busy this afternoon."

Karen's Cast

"Hey, everybody!" I called when we got home. "Elizabeth! Kristy! Charlie! Sa — "

"Karen, don't shout so," said Daddy.

"But this is important," I told him. "I need people to sign my cast."

"Well, go find them, honey," said Daddy. "Look. Here's a red pen." He pulled a pen out of his shirt pocket and gave it to me. "Take this with you. Just calm down. There's no reason to yell."

I tried to calm down. "Thank you," I said as I took the pen. I went out to our backyard.

Sam and Charlie were there. They were playing catch with David Michael.

"You guys! Hey, you guys!" I called. "Come here!"

"Why?" asked David Michael. He swung his bat and missed the ball. "Look at that! You made me miss!"

"Did not!" I cried. "Now come here. I want you to sign my cast."

"Really?" said David Michael. My brothers looked interested. They dropped their mitts and the bat and ball. They came over to me and I gave Sam my pen.

"Can you write your name or something funny or draw a picture?" I asked him as I took off my sling.

"Sure," replied Sam. He thought for a moment. Then he wrote,

Yours till the banana
splits. Ha, ha, ha! Sam

I giggled.

Sam gave the pen to Charlie, and Charlie wrote,

> Roses are red,
> cabbages are green,
> my face is funny,
> but yours is a scream.
> Your brother Charlie.

I stuck my tongue out at him. But I could not help laughing.

"David Michael?" I asked.

David Michael looked very thoughtful.
After a long pause he wrote,

GET WELL SOON.
DAVID MICHAEL THOMAS.

"That's great!" I cried. "Thanks, you guys.
By the way, do you know anyone famous?"

My brothers shook their heads. I went
looking for the rest of my family.

First I found Kristy, and she wrote,

Roses are red,
violets are blue.
sugar is sweet,
and so are you!
Love, Kristy

Then I found Andrew, and he wrote,

ANDREW

Then I found Daddy, and he wrote,

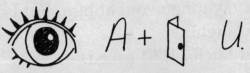

The autographs were great, but Daddy did not know anyone famous. Neither did Kristy or Andrew.

At last I found Elizabeth. I gave her the red pen. She wrote,

YOURS TILL ICE SCREAMS!
LOVE, ELIZABETH

"Thank you," I said. "Do you know anyone famous?"

Elizabeth frowned. "I don't think so, honey. Why?"

I told her about Ricky and his cast and Hubert Gregory.

"Oh," said Elizabeth. "I see." She paused. "Hey, I've got an idea! Come with me. And take off your sling on the way."

I followed Elizabeth into the den. First she got an ink pad. Then she got some tissues. Then she tiptoed over to the couch. Shannon and Boo-Boo were lying there. They were napping.

Very carefully, Elizabeth lifted Boo-Boo's

front paw. She opened the ink pad and pressed Boo-Boo's foot onto it.

"HISSSSSS!" went Boo-Boo. He did not like being disturbed.

But quick as a flash, Elizabeth put Boo-Boo's foot on my cast. It left a pawprint!

"There's Boo-Boo's autograph," she said, as she cleaned up his foot. "Boo-Boo isn't famous, but this is a pretty special autograph."

I smiled at Boo-Boo's pawprint.

Then Elizabeth got Shannon's autograph the same way — except that Shannon slept through the whole thing.

Two pawprints. "Thanks!" I cried. "That's neat, Elizabeth!"

Only I knew that the pawprints were not *quite* as good as Hubert Gregory's signature. They were good — but not good enough.

I still needed a really really really special autograph.

Where would I get it?

Karen's Story Grows

I decided I would have to go visiting. I needed lots of people to sign my cast, anyway. I would ask our neighbors to do it. Then I would ask them if they knew anyone famous.

"Elizabeth? May I go over to Hannie's? And then maybe to Amanda Delaney's? I need some more autographs on my cast."

"Sure," replied Elizabeth. "Just be careful. And come home if you're tired or if your arm starts to hurt."

"Okay. Thanks!"

I ran across the street to the Papadakises' house. Hannie and her family had been away the day before. Boy, would Hannie be surprised when she saw me.

"Karen!" Hannie cried when she opened her door. "What happened?"

"I broke my wrist," I said proudly.

"Hey, everyone! Come here!" Hannie called.

Hannie's parents and her brother, Linny, came running. They all wanted to hear about my accident. So I told them the story.

"I was showing Andrew a new trick," I said. But suddenly, five coffee cans didn't sound like enough. Not enough for a broken wrist, anyway. "I lined up seven coffee cans on the sidewalk," I went on. "Then I backed way, way up. I skated toward those cans so fast I was almost flying. I sailed over them. . . . I *was* flying! Just for a second. And I did a triple twist in the air. Then I landed."

"And that's when you fell?" asked Linny.

"Nope. Not then," I said. "I landed perfectly. But right in front of me I saw a mother caterpillar and her three babies." Yeah! That sounded pretty good. "I didn't want to squish the babies, so I tried to jump over them, too. *That* was when I fell." (Mr. and Mrs. Papadakis frowned, but they did not say anything.)

"Did you fall on the caterpillars?" asked Hannie.

"What? Oh. Oh, no. They were safe," I said quickly. "Would you like to sign my cast? All of you? I need autographs on it. Look, even Shannon and Boo-Boo have signed it." I took off my sling and held out my arm so the Papadakises could look at the cast.

"I'll go get a pen!" Hannie cried.

"Get one that isn't red," I told her. I wanted my cast to look as colorful as Ricky's.

Hannie and Linny and their mother and father signed my cast.

"I guess Sari is too little to sign it, isn't she?" I said. (Sari is the littlest Papadakis.)

"Yes," agreed Mrs. Papadakis. "But how would you like another pawprint? I think we could get Noodle's autograph." (Noodle is a poodle.)

"Thank you very much," I said when Noodle was finished. "By the way, does anyone here know a famous person?"

"No," said Hannie and Linny.

"I know the dogcatcher," said Mr. Papadakis.

I shook my head.

"I know the mayor," said Mrs. Papadakis.

"You *do?*" I cried. "Could he sign my cast? I need a famous autograph before tomorrow."

"Oh," said Hannie's mother. "I'm sorry, Karen. He's not in town this weekend."

"That's okay," I answered in a teeny-tiny voice.

"Hey, Karen! How about a *claw*print? That would be good!" exclaimed Hannie. "We'll get Myrtle to sign your cast. A turtle's autograph!"

It wasn't easy, but Hannie and Linny put Myrtle's clawprint on my cast.

When they were done, I said, "Thanks, everybody. I have to go now. I'm going to ask some more people to sign my cast. Want to come with me, Hannie?"

"Where are you going first?"

"Over to Amanda Delaney's."

"Karen Brewer! How could you do that to me?" Hannie cried. "You know Amanda and I are VERY BIG ENEMIES!"

Karen's Story Grows
Some More

Hannie Papadakis hardly ever gets mad. She hardly ever yells. But it is true. She does not like Amanda. And Amanda does not like her. Amanda can make Hannie mad.

"I'm sorry, Hannie," I said. "I need Amanda to sign my cast. And Max and their mom and dad."

Hannie was walking me to the front door. "Well, I am not going!" she said.

I began to feel mad, too. "Okay! Then don't!"

"I won't!"

"Good!"

"Good-bye!"

"GOOD-BYE!"

I stomped over to the Delaneys' house. *Stomp, stomp, stomp.* Each time I stomped, I felt a little less angry. By the time I rang Amanda's door, I was not angry at all. I even wished Hannie had come with me. It's very silly of her not to like Amanda. And it's silly of Amanda not to like Hannie.

When I rang Amanda's bell, Shannon Kilbourne answered the door. Shannon lives in the house between Hannie and Amanda. Shannon is a baby-sitter, just like Kristy. (She gave us our dog, and that's why we named the puppy Shannon. For Shannon Kilbourne.)

"Hi, Shannon," I said. "Are you baby-sitting for Amanda and Max?"

"Yes, I am. Karen, what happened to your arm?" Shannon asked.

So I had to tell the story again. Shannon invited me into Amanda and Max's play-

room, and I told them how I had jumped over ten coffee cans. And how I had broken my wrist and the police had had to come. An ambulance, too.

I just love telling stories. And this one was getting to be one of my best. No one would ever know that I had fallen just by trying to turn around.

When I was finished, I said, "Will you sign my cast?"

"Sure," replied Amanda and Max and Shannon.

Amanda wrote:

Read	see	that	me.
up	will	I	love
and	you	love	you
down	and	you	and

"Neat!" I cried.

Then Shannon wrote,

Best wishes from
Shannon Kilbourne

And Max, who is six, wrote,

Hi FROM MAX.

"Thanks," I said. "By the way, Shannon and Boo-Boo and Noodle put their paw-prints on my cast. And Myrtle put her clawprint on it. Maybe Priscilla could sign my cast, too." Priscilla is the Delaneys' fluffy white cat.

"How did you get their pawprints?" asked Amanda.

"With an ink pad," I told her.

"Ink? No way! I do not want Priscilla's paw to get dirty."

I sighed. "Okay," I said. "Hey, do you guys know anyone famous?"

"Why?" asked Shannon.

"I need someone famous to sign my cast," I answered. "By tomorrow. It's important."

"I don't know anyone," said Amanda.

"Me neither," said Shannon.

But Max said, "This boy in my class? Well, he has an aunt who has a friend who goes to this hairdresser. And this hairdresser once cut Frances Morton's hair."

"Who is Frances Morton?" I asked.

"A singer," said Max. "I think."

"Are you sure the hairdresser cut her hair?"

"No," admitted Max.

"Well," I said, "thank you. But your friend probably couldn't sign my cast before tomorrow. Besides, it would be better if Frances Morton could sign my cast herself."

"Hey!" Amanda shouted. "Guess what! I hear bells! Mr. Tastee is coming!"

Mr. Tastee

"Hooray!" I cried. "The ice-cream man! And I have fifty cents with me!"

"Can we have ice-cream money, Shannon?" asked Amanda.

And Max added, "Puh-*lease?*"

Shannon gave Amanda and Max some money and we ran across the Delaneys' lawn. We stopped at the sidewalk. We could see Mr. Tastee's truck a few houses away. We could hear it, too. The bells were ringing and music was playing. Across the street, the door to my house opened. Andrew and

David Michael ran out. I knew they had ice-cream money, too.

Then Hannie and Linny joined us. Hannie might not like Amanda. But she likes ice cream. A lot. So she stood with us.

"Are you mad at me?" I whispered to Hannie.

"Not really," she replied. "Are you mad at me?"

"Nope."

We smiled at each other.

Mr. Tastee drove slowly down the street. Just in case he didn't see us, we all began waving our arms. We yelled, "Stop! Stop here, Mr. Tastee!"

Jangle, jangle went the bells. The truck stopped right beside us. Mr. Tastee stepped out.

"Karen Brewer!" he exclaimed. "What on earth did you do to yourself?"

I giggled. Mr. Tastee is really nice. He cares about us kids. He always stops and talks to us. We just love Mr. Tastee.

I told Mr. Tastee how I broke my wrist. I

told him an even better story than I'd told Shannon and Amanda and Max. The new story had helicopters and fire engines in it. When I got to that part, I realized something. Everyone was staring at me. Mr. Tastee's mouth was open. "Karen," he said, "are you *sure* that's what happened?"

"No, it is not!" Andrew spoke up. "That is a very big story. There were only two coffee cans. And there were no caterpillars or ambulances or police cars or fire engines or helicopters."

Now everyone was staring at Andrew. He hardly ever talks so much.

At last Amanda said, "Why don't you tell us the truth, Karen?"

So I did. It wasn't nearly as interesting, but nobody seemed to mind. And nobody laughed at me. They were much more interested in my cast and in the autographs than in how I'd fallen.

Then I said, "Mr. Tastee, could I have a Fudgsicle, please?"

Andrew asked for a Sno-Kone, David

Michael asked for an Italian ice, Hannie and Linny asked for chocolate ice-cream cones, and Amanda and Max asked for Creamsicles.

We paid Mr. Tastee. Just before he climbed back in his truck, I got an idea.

"Mr. Tastee, would you sign my cast, please?" I asked him.

Mr. Tastee found a pen. He wrote,

TO KAREN,
ONE OF MY BEST CUSTOMERS.
BEST WISHES,
ROGER JONES

"Roger Jones!" I cried. "Don't you mean
. . . Isn't your name Mr. Tastee?"

"Roger Tastee?" asked Mr. Tastee. He
was smiling. "I'm sorry, Karen. Mr. Tastee
is just the name of the ice-cream company."

"Oh." I blushed. Then I said, "Could you
maybe write 'Mr. Tastee' underneath your
name? Just so people will know who Roger
Jones is?" I asked.

"Okay," said Mr. Tastee. He got his pen
out again. "There you go." Then he climbed
in his truck and drove off.

My friends and brothers and I looked at
each other. We could not believe that Mr.
Tastee was really Roger Jones.

And I said, "Boo. I still don't have a
special autograph."

"What about Mr. Tastee's?" said David Michael.

I frowned. "I'm not sure. Ricky might have his, too. And *darn it*. I forgot to ask Mr. Tastee if he knows anyone famous."

The afternoon was not going as well as I wanted it to.

I needed to do some thinking.

Eek! Morbidda Destiny!

My friends and brothers and I sat down on the curb. We licked our Mr. Tastee treats. As we sat, I thought.

I looked across the street. I saw the place where I had fallen. I saw our garage, where my skates were. They would be stuck in the garage for weeks and weeks. Then I saw . . . Morbidda Destiny, the witch next door!

"Eek! There's Morbidda Destiny!" I whispered loudly.

Everyone looked over at her house.

"I bet she's gathering herbs for a spell," I said softly.

"What kind of spell?" asked Andrew. His voice was trembling.

"I don't know. Something awful. Maybe a spell to take away Christmas."

"A spell to take away *Christ*mas?" howled Max. "No!"

"SHH!" I said. "Boy, isn't it just my luck that I have to live next door to a witch? I'm sure she's the only witch in town. And she lives — Hey! That's it!" I cried. Then I lowered my voice. I didn't want the witch to hear me. "That's it," I said more softly.

"That's what?" asked David Michael.

"Nothing," I answered. I was busy thinking. I could get Morbidda Destiny to sign my cast. Ricky wouldn't have a *witch's* autograph. And a witch's autograph would be better than Hubert Gregory's any day.

Hmm. How would I *get* the witch's autograph, though? I would have to go to her house, or at least into her yard. I would have to stand near her. She would have to touch my cast. Was I brave enough for all that?

Of course I was. . . . Well, I would be, if someone came with me. Someone like Hannie Papadakis. That was all I needed — a friend.

"Hannie?" I said. "Want to come over for awhile?"

"Sure," replied Hannie. I could tell she

was glad I hadn't asked Amanda to come over, too.

Hannie and I stood up. We were still licking our ice creams.

"See you guys later," I said.

"See you," said Andrew, David Michael, Linny, Max, and Amanda.

"I'm glad you're not mad at me anymore," I said to Hannie as we crossed the street.

"I'm glad, too," replied Hannie.

"Since we're friends again, will you help me with something?"

"What do you need help with?" asked Hannie.

"I want you to come over to Morbidda Destiny's with me."

Lucky Charms

"N o!" cried Hannie. Then she whispered, "I am *not* going to the witch's house again. The last time we went over there we got into very big trouble."

That was true. But that was because we did something wrong. "We won't do anything wrong this time," I told Hannie. We reached my house. We let ourselves inside and went to my room. "In fact, we're going to do something nice. We're going to ask Mor — Mrs. Porter for her autograph. Don't you think that will make her happy? She will think we like her. We won't get in trouble for that."

"We-ell," said Hannie slowly. "But aren't you afraid of her, Karen? I am. She's a witch."

"I know. But I think we'll be safe. If we go over soon, she'll still be outside in her garden. She couldn't hurt us then."

"Why not?" asked Hannie.

"Because everyone would see. Andrew and David Michael and Linny and Max and Amanda are right across the street. The witch won't do anything with people watching. I know she won't."

"Maybe not," said Hannie.

"Don't you want me to have the best cast in our class tomorrow?" I asked.

"Yes."

"Then will you help me?"

Hannie sighed. "Yes."

"Okay, now we have to think about how we're going to ask Morbidda Destiny for her autograph."

"Can't you just say, 'Please sign my cast'?" suggested Hannie.

"What if she wants to know *why* I want her to sign my cast? I can't tell her it's because she's a witch."

"Then say it's because . . . it's because . . . Oh, I don't know, Karen. You'll think of something won't you?"

"I guess so," I replied. I usually do.

"I don't know why I'm helping you," said Hannie. She made a face.

"I do. Because you're my friend."

Hannie and I smiled at each other.

"Now," I said, "we better protect ourselves while we're next door. We need some lucky charms. Just in case. I'll put my lucky rabbit's foot in my pocket. And you can put

. . . let's see. You can put my lucky stone in your pocket."

The stone I keep in my bureau drawer isn't really lucky. It's just pretty, but if Hannie *believed* it was lucky, that was probably all that mattered. So I told her it was a lucky stone. "Then we'll be safe," I added. I gave Hannie the stone. "Ready?" I asked.

"I hope so," Hannie replied.

The Witch's Autograph

Hannie and I finished our ice creams. I threw the stick away. Then we left our house. My hand was closed around the rabbit's foot. Hannie's was closed around the stone.

"Keep your hand on the stone all the time," I warned Hannie. "I'll keep — Uh-oh." I looked around nervously.

"What's wrong?" asked Hannie in a squeaky voice.

"That." I pointed to Morbidda Destiny's

garden. It was empty. "She's gone," I said. "She's probably inside now. We'll have to ring her doorbell."

"Noooo."

"It's the only thing, Hannie. Look. Everybody is still outside. And Shannon's with them now. We'll be safe. So we'll ring the witch's doorbell. Then we'll stand on her porch and when she answers the door, I'll ask for her autograph. Simple. We won't go inside or anything."

"All right."

We walked out of my yard. We walked into Morbidda Destiny's. Her big old house stood before us. Very slowly, we climbed the porch steps. I looked at Hannie. Her hand was still in her pocket. "Are you holding the stone?" I asked.

She nodded.

"Good. Hold it tight. I'm holding the rabbit's foot. Our lucky charms will protect us."

I rang Morbidda Destiny's doorbell. My hand was shaking.

After a moment, Hannie and I heard footsteps inside.

"Yes?" called a wobbly voice.

"It's us!" I said. "It's Karen Brewer and Hannie Papadakis."

The door opened slightly. Hannie and I could see a squinty eye and a pointy nose.

Then the door opened the rest of the way.

There stood my witch. She looked the same as always. She was wearing a long black dress. It came right to the tops of her black shoes. Her gray hair was flying every which way.

"Well," she said, "what can I do for you girls?"

I took off my sling and held out my arm. "I broke my wrist," I said timidly. "Would you, um, would you please sign my cast?"

"How did you break it?" Morbidda Destiny asked.

"I was skating and I fell down," I told her.

The witch nodded. She did not look impressed.

"I know it isn't very interesting," I said, "but that's what happened."

"Why do you want my autograph?" asked Morbidda Destiny.

Hannie and I glanced at each other.

"Because you're my neighbor," I said. I said it just as Hannie said, "Because she's in a cast-signing contest."

Morbidda Destiny looked confused, but all she said was, "Let's see here." She reached into the folds of her dress. Like magic, she pulled out a pen. Where had that pen been hiding?

The witch reached for my arm. I squinched my eyes shut. I felt like I was at the doctor's, waiting for a shot. Suddenly I was terrified. What was I doing? Was I crazy, letting a witch sign my cast? Maybe if I pulled my arm away right then —

"There we go!" exclaimed Morbidda Destiny. She smiled happily.

Oh, no! She had already signed my cast! I dared to open my eyes. What would I see? What would a witch put on a cast?

In big black letters were the words "Tabitha Porter." Next to them was a drawing of a black cat. A black cat! Why had she drawn that? What was it? A spell? Maybe it was an awful sign that would attract other witches. What a horrible thought. But I couldn't do anything about it.

I had a witch name and a witch cat on my cast now. It was time to go.

"Th-thanks, Mrs. Porter!" I cried.

Then I grabbed Hannie's hand and we ran to my house.

Home Safely

Hannie and I slammed the front door behind us. We were breathing very hard. We didn't say a word. After a few moments, I went into the living room. I turned on a light. I was going to examine what Morbidda Destiny had written.

Just then I heard Charlie call, "Karen? Is that you?"

"Yes!" I yelled back. I was shaking. But I said to Hannie, "Let's show everyone the witch's autograph." If no one else seemed worried about the black cat, then I wouldn't be worried either, I decided.

I found my big brothers in the kitchen, eating.

They are always eating.

"Look! Mrs. Porter signed my cast!" I said.

Charlie smiled.

Sam said, "Big deal."

Hannie and I went into the backyard. Daddy and Elizabeth were gardening. Kristy was helping them. "Look!" I said again. "Mrs. Porter signed my cast!"

Daddy and Elizabeth and Kristy put down their trowels. They took off their gardening gloves. Then they stood up.

"You guys went over to Mrs. Porter's?" exclaimed Kristy. "I thought you were afraid of her."

Daddy and Elizabeth were peering at my cast.

"Very nice," said Daddy. "She even drew a picture of Midnight."

TABITHA PORTER

Oh! Midnight! So that's what the picture was. I felt very silly . . . and very relieved.

"I'm sure Mrs. Porter was happy that you wanted her autograph," added Elizabeth. "She's so lonely. Visits from kids must mean a lot to her."

"Well, really," Hannie began, "we needed the autograph of a wi — "

"Of all our neighbors," I interrupted loudly. Daddy and Elizabeth would not be happy if they knew Hannie and I were calling Mrs. Porter a witch again. "Come on, Hannie. Let's go count my autographs."

I pulled Hannie into the house. Whew!

"Hannie," I said, "you can't tell grown-ups about witches. Especially about Mrs.

Porter. They don't understand."

"Oh," replied Hannie.

We went back to the lamp in the living room.

"Tabitha Porter," I said, looking at the autograph. "A witchy-sounding name. Still, I wish Mrs. Porter had written 'Morbidda Destiny' so everyone would know it was the autograph of my witch."

"Well, I will tell them," said Hannie. "I was with you. I know."

"Thank you," I replied.

I was happy at last. Maybe my cast wouldn't be better than Ricky's, but it would be just as good.

Good-byes and Hellos

"K aren!" Kristy called.

"What?" I shouted. Hannie and I were still in the living room. We had been counting autographs.

"It's time for you and Andrew to get ready to go home."

"All right," I said. I sighed. I had lost count.

So had Hannie. She decided to leave.

" 'Bye!" I called. "See you in school tomorrow. Thank you for helping me."

Kristy found Andrew outside. She brought

him in. Then she brought both of us upstairs to get ready to go back to Mommy's. Kristy likes to help Andrew and me. We have special good-bye visits with her. First she talks to Andrew while she helps him. Then she talks to me. I do not need any help, though.

"What a weekend, Karen," said Kristy as she came into my room.

"It was exciting, wasn't it?" I replied.

Kristy laughed. "I'll say! Think of everything that happened."

"I got a witch's autograph."

"You got a witch's autograph?! How about having an accident? Breaking your wrist? And going to the hospital — twice?"

"Getting X rays," I added. "Meeting Tom. Meeting a bone doctor. Riding in a wheelchair. And seeing Ricky and *his* cast."

"Right," said Kristy. "But you know what? I hope we don't have this kind of excitement too often."

"I wouldn't mind. When I go to school tomorrow, I will be a star."

"You will be a co-star," Kristy reminded me. "Ricky will have a cast, too, so he will be another star."

"Yeah. Darn old Ricky."

"Come on," said Kristy. "Your mom will be here any minute."

Andrew and I got our knapsacks. We went downstairs to wait. Soon, Mommy and Seth drove into Daddy's driveway.

"Good-bye! Good-bye!" Andrew and I

called to Daddy and Elizabeth and Kristy and Sam and Charlie and David Michael and Shannon and Boo-Boo. It took us a long time to hug everybody.

Then we ran to Mommy and Seth. "Hello! Hello!" we called. We kissed them as we climbed into the car. Their car was full of suitcases and things from their trip to the state of Maine.

"My poor Karen!" exclaimed Mommy when she saw my cast and sling.

"My arm hardly hurts at all," I told her. "And look. Look at all the autographs on my cast. Now you and Seth have to sign it."

Mommy was driving, so Seth signed my cast. He wrote

U R 2 nice
2 B 4- gotten.
Love,
Seth

Mommy said, "I'll sign your cast at home, honey. Hey, how would you like the autograph of a famous person? My friend Amy

Morris is in Stoneybrook this weekend. Maybe we could visit her tonight."

"Amy Morris the movie star?!" I shrieked. "She's a friend of yours? And she's *here?*"

"Yes," said Mommy, laughing.

I could not believe it. I just could not believe it. I went looking for someone famous and did not find anybody. Then I stopped looking and found somebody. Oh, well. Whether we saw Amy Morris or not, I would still be the only kid with a witch's autograph.

I smiled. It had not been such a bad weekend after all.

L. GODWIN

About the Author

ANN M. MARTIN lives in New York City and loves animals, especially cats. She has three cats of her own, Gussie, Woody, and Willy, and one dog, Sadie.

Other books by Ann M. Martin that you might enjoy are *Stage Fright, Me and Katie (the Pest)*, and the books in *The Baby-Sitters Club* series.

Ann likes ice cream and *I Love Lucy*. And she has her own little sister, whose name is Jane.